Querido dragón pasa el día con papá

Dear Dragon's Day with Father

por/by Margaret Hillert

ilustrado por/Illustrated by David Schimmell

NORWOOD HOUSE PRESS

Norwood House Press • P.O. Box 316598 • Chicago, Illinois 60631
For more information about Norwood House Press please visit our website at
www.norwoodhousepress.com or call 866-565-2900.
Text copyright ©2010 by Margaret Hillert. Illustrations and cover design copyright ©2010 by Norwood House Press, Inc. All rights reserved. No part of this book may be reproduced or utilized in any form or by any means without written permission from the publisher.
Designer: The Design Lab

LIBRARY OF CONGRESS CATALOGING-IN-PUBLICATION DATA
  Hillert, Margaret.
    [Dear dragon's day with father. Spanish & English]
    Querido dragon pasa el dia con papa = Dear dragon's day with father / por
  Margaret Hillert ; ilustrado por David Schimmell ; traducido por Eida Del Risco.
      p. cm. — (A beginning-to-read book)
    Summary: "A boy and his pet dragon spend a day participating in activities
  with the boy's father"—Provided by publisher.
      ISBN-13: 978-1-59953-360-5 (library edition : alk. paper)
      ISBN-10: 1-59953-360-X (library edition : alk. paper)
    [1. Dragons—Fiction. 2. Fathers and sons—Fiction. 3. Spanish language materials—Bilingual.] I.
  Schimmell, David, ill. II. Del Risco, Eida. III.Title. IV. Title: Dear dragon's day with father.
    PZ73.H557210 2010
    [E]—dc22
                          2009041521

Manufactured in the United States of America in North Mankato, Minnesota.
160N-072010

Papá, papá.
¿Puedes venir?
Tengo algo para ti.

Father, Father.
Can you come here?
I have something for you.

Estoy aquí.
¿Qué tienes para mí?
Lo quiero ver.

Here I am.
What do you have for me?
I want to see it.

Huy,
qué linda es.
Me la voy a poner.
Me gusta.

Oh, my.
How pretty it is.
I will put it on.
I like it.

Te queda bien.
Eres un buen papá.
Trabajas para traer dinero a casa.
¿Podemos ver dónde trabajas?

It looks good on you.
And you are a good father.
You go to work for us.
Can we go to see where you work?

Sí, sí.
Pueden ver donde trabajo.

Yes, yes.
You can see where I work.

¿Podemos subir al auto?
¿Podemos ir ahora, papá?
¿Podemos ir contigo al trabajo?

Can we get in the car?
Can we go now, Father?
Can we go to work with you?

Sí. Sí.
Suban. Suban.
Ahora nos vamos.

Yes. Yes.
Get in. Get in.
Now we will go.

Nos vamos.
Lejos, lejos, lejos.

Away we go.
Away, away, away.

Ya llegamos. Este es el lugar.
Aquí es donde trabaja papá.

Here we are. This is the spot.
Here is where Father works.

Tenemos que subir. ¡Arriba, arriba, ARRIBA!

We have to go up. Up, up, UP!

Mira afuera. Oh, mira allá afuera.
Mira a lo lejos.
¿Qué ves?

Look out here. Oh, look out here.
Look way, way out.
What do you see?

¿Y aquí es donde trabajas?
Parece un buen lugar.

And this is where you work?
It looks like a good spot.

Sí, aquí es donde trabajo.
Es bueno trabajar,
pero también es bueno divertirse.
Ahora podemos ir a algún lugar
a divertirnos.

Yes, this is where I work.
It is good to work
but it is good to have fun, too.
Now we can go somewhere
to have fun.

Llegamos.
Este es el lugar.
Salgan. Salgan.

Here we are.
This is the spot.
Get out. Get out.

Pon esto ahí.
Alguno lo va a querer.
Alguno se lo va a comer.

Put this down here.
Something will want it.
Something will come to eat it.

Veo algo. Ay, ay, ay.
Mira eso.

I see something. Oh, oh, oh.
Look at that.

Mira lo que tengo.
Ay, mira lo que tengo.
Es uno grande.

Look what I have.
Oh, look what I have.
It is a big one.

Tú tienes uno. Y tú también.
Ahora son tres. Uno, dos, tres.

You have one, too. And so do you.
That makes three. One, two, three.

Ahora los pueden soltar.
Tenemos que irnos.
Suban al auto y nos vamos.

Now let them go.
We have to go.
Get in the car and we will go.

Ya llegamos, mamá.
Ya llegamos.
Fue un buen día.

Here we are, Mother.
Here we are.
It was a good day.

Eso me alegra.
Ahora podemos hacer
algo de comer.
Qué bueno.

That makes me happy.
Now we can make
something to eat.
That will be good.

Tú estás conmigo
y yo estoy contigo.
Ay, qué día más alegre con papá,
querido dragón.

Here you are with me.
And here I am with you.
Oh, what a happy day with Father,
dear dragon.

READING REINFORCEMENT

The following activities support the findings of the National Reading Panel that determined the most effective components for reading instruction are: Phonemic Awareness, Phonics, Vocabulary, Fluency, and Text Comprehension.

Phonemic Awareness: Rhyming Words

1. Say the following groups of three words and ask your child to tell you which two of the words rhyme:

cart, part, port	four, pair, stare	dirt, hurt, dart
bear, chair, bar	car, far, fur	core, care, store
park, dark, pork	skirt, start, shirt	shore, share, more

Phonics: r-controlled Vowels

1. Explain to your child that sometimes, the letter **r** after a vowel changes the sound of the vowel (for example, cat/cart).

2. Make four columns on a blank sheet of paper and label each with the following r-controlled vowel sample words: car, father, fork, air.

3. Write the following words on separate index cards:

far	work	horse	hair	barn	bird	north
care	jar	river	morning	bear	park	mother

4. Mix the cards up well. These lists are arranged according to vowel sounds to help you check the sorting activity that follows.

5. Ask your child to select a card. Read each word aloud or ask your child to read it and place the card under the word that represents the r-controlled vowel sound in the word.

Vocabulary: Story-related Words

1. Write the following words on sticky note paper and point to them as you read them to your child:

    necktie   briefcase   skyscraper   elevator

2. Mix the words up. Say each word in random order and ask your child to point to the correct word as you say it.